RALPH & MURRAY

RICK GLAZE

SCREENSHOT
PUBLISHERS

ScreenShot Publishers

Nashville, TN

650-492-0920

Ricksbooks@rickglaze.com

ScreenShot Publishers

Cover illustration & Design/Map: Scott Simpson

Editing: Stephanie Parent, Sam Severn

ISBN 978-1-7372951-2-9 eBook

ISBN 978-1-7372951-3-6 Paperback

ISBN 978-1-7372951-4-3 Audio Book

DEDICATION

If you don't already know where this book takes place by the streets you grew up in, look at the exact center of Tennessee on your map and you'll see this quaint little hamlet that has grown into a sprawling and vibrant town. From the 1950s town of Murfreesboro, where there was never a need to lock your doors, I thank all my friends and family who joined me in an idyllic childhood.

Special thanks to Buddy Elrod for reminding me of and embellishing some of these stories that may have happened more like Ralph tells it than Buddy remembers it. Just Sayin'. Thanks to Betty Price who truly loves Ralph and is graciously tolerant of Murray...who could blame her. A special shoutout to my brother Tommy.

A very special thanks to the readers of this book. I hope you get a lot of laughs and maybe a few insightful moments. Let me hear your thoughts on RickGlaze.com.

This book is dedicated to my parents, Kay and Helen. How could anybody luck into better parents.

PREMIUM READER CLUB

Rick's Premium Reader Club members get free books, free behind the scenes photos, original songs written for the books and more. Members are always first to hear about new offerings and publications. Join the fun!

Visit www.RickGlaze.com

ALSO BY RICK GLAZE

Books

Spanish Pieces of Eight

The Purple River

Jackass: A Short Story Collection

Music CDs

Anegada Caribbean Breeze

Silicon Cowboy

www.RickGlaze.com

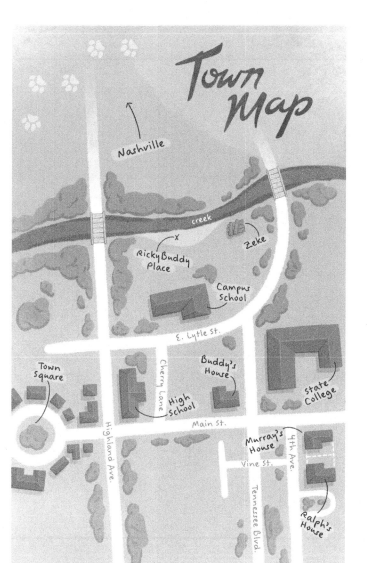

CONTENTS

CHAPTER 1

RALPH & MURRAY

After the car ride across town when they first brought me home, my stomach was rumbling around, and I up-chucked on the kitchen floor. That's when they named me Ralph. It's an average name for a dog. Especially suited for a pound-puppy with short, white hair from the neck down, black and brown fur on my head distributed judiciously, lanky legs not quite eight inches long, and a nondescript tail wagging most of the time. I lie around the house and yard like dogs tend to do, waiting on some action from the people around here.

A cat started wandering over my fence and I raced out and pretended to catch him in my lock-jaw fangs and tear him to shreds. Actually, it's Murray next door and if he didn't show up occasionally, it would be even more boring when the kids are off at school. So, I race out to intercept him, he screeches and arches his back and pretends he's a vicious lion, and king of the fence. We have a Mexican standoff for a minute from his perch on top of the fence; then he jumps back to his yard and I go back to the shade of my patio. It breaks up the afternoon, what can I say?

Like most Americans, I don't have a notable pedigree. And no, I don't try to fabricate the pedigree thing by showing off "designer" labels. Well, I actually don't wear labels. But if I had a well-placed blush of color across my back, I might have a pedigree...at least for some folks. It's a fun game, but actually I have more fun with the Murray thing.

WHEN I JOINED THE FAMILY, Tommy was eleven, and Ricky was nine. I was almost six months old and didn't know much about a dog's life or how people acted, but I started watching everything. I noticed there was a hierarchy in the family, a kind of pecking order, and it adjusted itself depending on who was in the house. For example, when Dad was home, there was an unwritten deferral to him as the top-dog, no pun intended. Mom was the default when Dad was on a trip, and when in their rooms, big brother Tommy was the alpha, leaving Ricky on the bottom rung...except for me, but I'm just a dog.

So telling a story from a dog's perspective, you'd think it would be pretty limited. After all, I can't speak, and I don't have a place at the supper table to talk over the day's events, and all that sort of thing. But two things happened that changed all that.

One April afternoon when the springtime sun was breaking through a cloudy gloom, and drying the winter-soaked yard, I was making a security check around the periphery of the back fence. I turned the corner and looked up to see Murray sitting leisurely on a cross beam at the top. He was sprawled out so his red-white-and-touches-of-black coat caught the waning sunlight in an almost shiny glisten. While standing there motionless dismissing my gut reaction to defend the sanctity of my turf, a small, quiet voice spoke into my ear. "How's it going today, buddy?" I tilted my head at this strange sound while I looked up at Murray. His mouth was stretched out in a big grin and it looked like he actually winked at me. Bewildered, my head turned back the other way. "It's okay, you can do this," the voice whispered. Looking back to Murray, I thought, "Are you talking to me?" "Yes, and it's okay," the voice said.

Over time, Murray showed me how to listen to everything around me including, and most intriguingly, people. When he climbs to the top of the fence, I still run out as if tearing him to pieces, because we both like doing it. But the world changed, and a lot of the things that happen are no longer a mystery.

Okay, as if that's not enough. In the evenings after dinner, the boys go to their rooms and do homework. As I had no homework of my own to do, I broke up the boredom by shuttling back and forth between the two bedrooms. Snuggling into Tom's bedspread, I watched him stare at books and quietly turn the pages, sometimes fast and other times deliberate, while writing on an adjacent pad. Watching Ricky was a different experience, and led to the second life-changing event. For one, he usually sat on the bed with a couple of pillows behind his back. Sometimes he had a pad of paper out, but other times he leafed through books with a steady even pace, and then I noticed the thing that was the defining moment. He was moving his lips as he read, literally mouthing the words. And get this, about half the time he actually whispered each word as he read...so low that people didn't notice, but I have better hearing than people. After a while I found a position to sit where I could watch the page while hearing the words. Now sit down and take a deep breath, because what I'm about to tell you is hard to swallow. Ready? Okay, here goes. Under this strange confluence of circumstances, I taught myself to read. Okay, I know. Believe me I get it. I'm a dog. Dogs can be very smart, and some can think and even outwit their masters. But read?

Well, let it settle in for a bit while I tell you some stories of growing up in this small Southern town.

CHAPTER 2
UNCLE BUCK

"Hey Murray, listen to this." Murray sat still and listened as he tuned into my thoughts. He turned his head and looked out toward the maple tree showing a slight grimace on his face.

"What is that? You sound like you have a stomach ache," Murray said.

"It's not a stomach ache, I'm singing. Ricky hums a tune almost all the time and sometimes just walks around singing one. I've been listening carefully and I picked up the melody for a few of them. I think I'm pretty dad-gum good."

"Ralph you're a great friend and a smart pooch, and you've picked up this special kind of talking we do, really quickly. You're very talented," Murray said. "But, Ralph, you can't sing. The people totally underestimate us and our abilities, it's true. Ralph, read my lips, oh I guess you can't read my lips 'cause

I'm not really moving my lips, but if you could, you would see that you're a dog and you can't sing."

"I think you're just jealous. Imagine a cat trying to sing! Your envy is as clear as that little black furry nose on your face. You're wallowing in it...a feline frenzy of envy," I retorted.

"Okay, Ralph. You win. But you still can't sing."

"Murray, you're really getting under my fur, but no hard feelings 'cause I feel a song coming on."

"I'm out of here," Murray said as he leaped off the fence and disappeared with a soft landing into his yard next door.

$\sim$

"THE BELCHORS ARE NICE NEIGHBORS. They're quiet, but nice," Mom said into the black cylinder that she held to her ear.

I learned it was called a telephone one night when she snapped at Ricky to 'get off the telephone, I'm expecting your grandmother to call from St. Louis.'

She continued on the phone, "Well I've invited them over for cocktails a couple of times, but they haven't accepted," she paused as she talked to her mother in St. Louis. "Yes, I see them in church some-times, but honestly I think they read and tend to their garden most of the time...he owns the hard-ware store on the square," she continued. "Honestly mom, I think they're homebodies and we should just let them be... Yes that little kitty is theirs. I forgot his name," she said into the phone.

I said 'Murray' to myself over a few times as loud as I could, which is my way of shouting. Then my mom looked down at me, paused, and said into the phone, "Murray, that's the name of the Belchor's cat."

$$\sim$$

THE FENCE between my house and the Belchor's was six feet high. Murray could jump up to the top, but I was relegated to viewing their yard through gaps between the boards, and a few chinks in the aging wood.

There was a chunk out just off the ground a little, where I could see the side of the house and the lavender and light-blue blossoms growing next to the red brick. They came out in the spring, and sometimes again in August, in a wet summer. My sense of smell is about a hundred times better than people, but even at that, these flowers didn't have a strong scent. One morning on the security check of my yard, I stopped to look through the chink into Murray's yard when I heard the familiar clunk of Murray landing on the top of the fence from a standing leap in his yard.

"Hydrangeas. That's what they're called," he said, up early interrupting my quiet, meditative morning.

"That's a big word for just a flower," I said.

"Mom was cutting some of them down when I heard Dad say, 'It's a good idea to thin out the hydrangeas.' That's how I learned the word," Murray said.

I kept looking through the chink and said, "Hey Murray, I can barely see some kind of tunnel in your back yard."

"It's kind of a tunnel, but it's called a trellis. It's a wood frame with vines growing on it that block out the sun in the afternoon. Dad built it and they both work on it, clipping, snipping, and in the fall it's almost like they cut it naked...I mean all the green is gone."

"Why do you think they work so hard on the green part, if it all falls off in the winter?" I asked.

"I really don't know. They don't do much in the winter they usually just sit in the living room quietly reading or talking," Murray said.

"Just the four of you?"

"Well, Jimmy is always in his room putting together a radio, train set, or other electronic gadget. So it's just the four of us."

"What do you mean four of you? I thought Jimmy was in his room," I said.

"Mom, Dad, me and Uncle Buck."

"Who is Uncle Buck?"

"Oh right. Uncle Buck stays on the mantle and I'll bet he gets kind of hot in the winter when that log fire is blazing," Murray said.

"Murray, have you been into the catnip lately. That doesn't make any sense," I said.

"Uncle Buck is in a blue and white urn on the mantel. They all got dressed up about five years ago, Mom was crying, Dad was stoned faced and Jimmy was staring out the window. When they got back, they put the urn on the mantel and it's been there ever since. Mom spent all day saying how nice the service was, and Dad said something about a funeral, but I can't figure out what a funeral means," Murray said.

"Does Uncle Buck talk or say anything?" I asked.

"Nothing yet. I thought about getting a little closer to his urn, but the jump to the mantel is a little dicey and if I don't hit it just right, Uncle Buck could be splattered all over the floor. And besides I might hit Muffy."

"Wait a minute; who's Muffy?" I said.

"He's the cat they had before me. He's in a little jar next to Uncle Buck."

THAT'S how it went when I first met Uncle Buck. My next story delves into the spirit world. 'That will be really fun,' you're thinking. Or, wait a minute, you may not believe in spirits. Either way, give this yarn a try. Sit back, loosen your collar and get ready for a fun summertime tale about old furniture, squirrels that talk and friendly ghosts. It's mostly at my expense, and I'm sure you'll develop a lot of sympathy for 'poor' Ralph as you plough through this story.

CHAPTER 3

STUCK IN THE GARAGE

The first peek of summer sun snuck through the floor-to-ceiling drapery as I opened one eye to the morning-after. I started out with my nose buried in the bedspread at Ricky's feet, moved to Mom and Dad's room and later wandered over to the couch in the den. Managing a slight roll to my side as my one open eye slammed shut, an eternity of 10 minutes dragged on until the smell of coffee woke me to the opportunities of the day. I walked over and waited by the door to the patio until Mom stopped by in a scurry and rolled the big glass door open for me.

Shuffling out the door to my patio-pillow, I plopped down, head extended over the edge, and watched in silence as the morning inched along. It was more mental than physical, but I was exhausted.

"So, where have you been? Martinique soaking up the rays? Maybe a day spa with designer soap and heat lamps in Memphis? Oh, and the food was probably lamb chops and ham hocks!"

I looked up to see Murray sitting on the fence with low morning-rays falling all over him like a summer leisure suit. The morning dew was vaporizing and filling the air with wafts of earthy aromas.

"What? Your mother never taught you any manners? You couldn't even say goodbye?" Murray continued.

"Cut it out Murray. I'm in no mood to spar and I have no cleverness this morning," I replied.

"Where have you been? He asked. "Don't tell me it's a long story."

I paused to gather my thoughts, "It's a short story with a long ending. Ricky and I were over on Tennessee Boulevard at Buddy's house. After we hung out upstairs for awhile, I followed them to that little dilapidated, well almost, garage. The stairs are in the back and we climbed those dusty steps to the storeroom. A powdery soot covered the floor, and the air was musty and 'old' smelling. Chairs, couches, floor-to-ceiling mirrors, bicycles, bird cages, you name it, they have at least one over there, covered in dust. I was making my way around through this menagerie when I heard the boys dart down the steps. I made a beeline over there just to see them run up again. They did it a couple of times and then I thought just let them play around till they're ready to go.

Then from behind one of the couches, I heard it. THE DOOR SLAM SHUT! When I got over there, it was latched tight and the boys were gone."

"You were stuck in that old dusty garage?" Murray asked.

"Stuck like glue! So I sniffed and pushed, then reached up for the knob, but nothing worked, so I settled into a spot right by the door," I said. "I guess it is normal to feel neglected."

"Neglected, abandoned, marooned! You were a castaway in a dust-filled funeral barge floating down the *River of Gloom*, discarded and forsaken!" Murray exclaimed.

Now these are the times that if you take Murray seriously, raw and as-is, it would be a tough pill to swallow, but I've learned to let those mutterings fall to the ground by their own weight, evaporate, and die unceremoniously. So, I continued.

"I knew they'd circle around the yard or cross Main Street to Johnny's Market for a popsicle and be back up there. But as the day retreated, I was getting a little worried. A few hours later I had to face the fact that they'd forgotten me. Surely Mom would figure this out and come to the rescue, but the hours ticked on and it was just me."

"Wow, sorry about the Martinique thing," Murray said.

"That's okay, I knew you were just exercising your twisted wit at my expense, as usual," I replied. "So Murray, a lot of things went through my mind that night. Some of them normal, like I wish Mom would heat up chicken broth and pour it on my dinner more often. But also some strange things. The most interesting thing was, I ran into a character named Buster."

"Buster? Who's that?" Murray asked.

"He's a squirrel, and he lives in a tree next to the house, and in his spare time he cruises around the second floor of the garage," I said.

"So cut to the chase. Did he show you the way out?" Murray asked.

"Of course he did."

"So you trotted on home and skipped Martinique, right?" Murray said, as he reached down to do a little cleaning of that red-tabby fur, making the black fur on the top of his head and ears bounce up and down like ping pong balls.

"Murray, sit back on your haunches and take your nose out of your furry stomach and listen carefully. I'm not a skinny little squirrel, or a smart-aleck little nebbish cat like you. Bottom line is, I couldn't fit through the worm-hole that Buster uses. Sure we tried a couple other exits, but no dice. I'm too big."

"So you were stuck there all night?" Murray asked.

"It got colder and quieter and I missed my family," I said.

"And you missed me, right?" Murray said.

"Not really, but the cool thing is, Buster showed me all around the place. He knows the names of all the people who slept in the beds, who sat at the desks and who rode some of the bikes," I said.

"Did he know all those people?" Murray asked.

"Heck no. Buster is around four years old. Some of those people passed on years ago." I said.

"Wow, interesting."

"Buster can see some of the people sitting at their desks or reading books," I said.

"Are they lost souls or ghosts or something?" Murray asked.

"No, Buster can see their energy and sometimes they talk to him. For instance Buster introduced me to Mr. Ellis Murfree sitting at his desk. He was a descendant of the founding family of the town. He never lived in that house but it was his desk that somehow ended up stored there. He just drops by sometimes to hangout.

"Did he tell you much about the other side of the veil? You know, after you die." Murray asked.

"Well...he said it was much more expansive and mostly gentler than on earth, but that some of the hard times here, and lessons he learned by solving those hardships pulled him up a rung on the evolutionary ladder. He was mellow and nonchalant about it all," I said.

"One thing I was wondering...did he move his lips when he talked to you?" Murray said.

"No, it was just like you and me. He thought it and I knew it," I said. "Oh and get this. The guy that built the place drops by sometimes. He had a trucking company and after his wife died he married the nursemaid, Abigail Winston, who was thirty years younger. His name was Ephram Hooper and he made a bundle with that trucking company."

I paused and then asked, "Hey Murray, what does 'a bundle' mean?"

"It's a kind of slang that people use to mean making a lot of money," he said.

"Buster was talking about it like somehow that made Ephram a special person. Is that the way people think?" I asked.

"Well they like to buy things and for some, buying things equals happiness and fulfillment."

"Did you talk to Ephram?" Murray asked.

"No he didn't show up last night, but I was sniffing around in this big wooden box full of books and saw a piece of paper with some writing on it. I knew it was numbers instead of words, but I couldn't understand them. When I looked up, there was a nice lady sitting on the edge of the box reading one of the books. I said hello, and after a few seconds she replied, but kept her head down looking at the book. When I asked her what the paper said, she replied that it was a budget for a picnic event at the hospital. Funny thing was, she didn't even look at the paper. And no, she didn't move her lips either."

"Boy oh boy, Ralph. You had a great time," Murray said.

"Buster told me she was here because part of the library from the old hospital was in that box."

"Another thing, Murray," I said. "The book she was reading was about you."

"You mean about a smart, vivacious, tabby cat with black and white tortoiseshell markings...oh and don't forget, loved by all?" Murray gushed.

"Well the front cover was hard to read in the dark but I think it said *Cat on a Hot Tin Roof*," I paused. "Murray, do we live in Tennessee?"

"I think so, why?"

"Because underneath the cat thing it said, Tennessee Williams."

"I'm not sure about that stuff. Next time my Mom settles into some quiet time, I'll ask her," Murray said.

HONESTLY, getting stuck for that long doesn't seem so bad now that it's over, and look what a good story it makes.

Now I have another story for you. There was plenty of kid-action around my house, but I'm not going to tell you about all of it. Gosh, that would fill up a library, but one of the stories was what they call life-threatening. After some help from Murray, I was able to contribute to keeping everybody safe.

This story is closer to a Maxwell Smart adventure than a Sherlock Holmes escapade. These are just kids though, and I'm just a dog. You were a kid once, and I'm sure you can relate. You'll have fun with this one.

CHAPTER 4

THE ROOF

S eeing Ricky and Buddy on the roof that afternoon wasn't a big deal because I'd seen the boys up there before. Tommy figured out how to jump from the ground up to the raised planter with the juniper bush in it, and then pull himself up to the roof. Dad let them do it, after all it was a relatively flat roof, but they always made sure Mom didn't see them. Dad had a free-spirit streak which everybody liked, but it didn't spill over into risking Mom's kids breaking their necks falling off a roof.

The boys were laughing, shuffling, and starting to play war games. I moved out of my shady perch into the sunlight so I could watch them.

Buddy, as best friend from down the street, was almost keeping up with Ricky chasing around on the roof from one side to the other.

"In-coming," Ricky yelled and ran over the top gable of the roof. Buddy followed and made the best "k'boom" sound he could, replicating an artillery blast from the enemy. The pretend explosion threw Ricky's whole body to the roof and Buddy, recognizing the danger dropped for cover and looked out over the yard for a possible air assault.

"Attack helicopters at three o'clock," Buddy yelled.

"Quick, grab the bazookas, let 'em have it before they make my wife a widow," Ricky screamed.

Buddy stopped and looked over at Ricky, paused for a split second to think this one over, then shouted, "Yeah, give 'em all we got. Blast those guys out of the sky."

This nine-year-old-boy-fantasy war went on for a good while but was slowing down when Buddy's foot snagged the edge of a shingle. His knee hit first as his elbow caught the weight of his body. Both hands reached out and grabbed, stopping his slide to the edge. Ricky hardly noticed, still defending the homeland from attack. Buddy worked his way to the top of the roof to pull himself up to his feet.

I caught a glimpse of Murray on the fence looking at me intensely. His thoughts were coming across and speaking into my ear.

"This doesn't look too good. Are you watching this?"

Now after all this time, I was well aware that Murray was a worrywart. Mostly I just let him rattle on about what bothered him, but this time I looked up at the boys, and while Ricky was elated and fearless, Buddy's face showed no sign of concern, but his thoughts were burning red-hot with caution, trepidation, and pure fear. His sight was blurring and his outsized feet were starting to drag and shuffle over the uneven, asphalt shingles.

I looked back at Murray and thought, "Yeah, I see it." "Well, do something. Something loud!" his voice rang out in my ear.

So I'm a dog right? I started barking. Barking and running back and forth in the yard far enough out to keep an eye on them. Mom came to the door, saw me and then in a scolding manner said, "Ralph, stop your barking and go lay down. You're bothering everybody." She turned on a dime and went back inside. I ran out and looked up again. I saw Ricky getting dis-oriented and Buddy's demeanor was straining.

I picked a straight line on the grass parallel to the roof and ran back and forth barking even louder. Mom rushed out into the yard looked up and saw the boys dart to the other side of the roof. She ran around the house to the other side, "Ricky get down from there right now! You boys get down."

They ran to the other side and got the same ultimatum. Buddy slowed down some, but nobody feigned a descent. Mom ran into the house for a few minutes then came back out yelling, "Ricky, Ricky." To no avail, until the blue Chevy Impala pulled into the driveway.

The exuberant grin left Ricky's face. Buddy's grin had long sense faded, but I could see gratitude and relief in his thoughts. Buddy's mother emerged from the car with a long finger pointing to the roof. Ordering them down was a mere formality because they knew who was in charge now. I ran to the other side of the house and saw Ricky lower himself to the planter-box, then a jump to the grass below. Buddy approached the edge of the roof, but his last step caught a roof tile and hurled him onto the shingles. He bounced once and then off the roof into the planter box. When his feet hit the ground his elbow was covered in mud and his forehead was scraped in two places.

As Buddy and his mother pulled out of the driveway, Murray caught my attention. "Nice work, Mr. Alert!" he said.

"Okay, you got that one right. Be nice, because I can still tear you to shreds with my steel-jaw." I replied.

"As if you could catch me." he said.

Okay, chalk one up for Murray.

THAT WAS ALL the excitement we needed for one afternoon. A lot of adventure happened in the summertime that was less treacherous. I had more time with Ricky and Tommy because they were out of school, and the days were longer. The boys were used to riding their bikes, wherever they wanted and mostly whenever they felt like it. The only rule was, be home for supper.

Moving on, I've been wanting to tell you about the secret fort...deep in the woods, hidden in a giant forest, where no grownups can go. It's an undercover hiding place for two boys and a precocious dog.

Well, I may be exaggerating a tiny bit. To be perfectly honest, it's really a grove of trees surrounding a small creek, across the street from Doctor Odell's office, a few hundred feet from Clark Boulevard. But, the whole 'deep in the woods' thing sounds pretty cool.

Oh yes, I almost forgot. You're going to meet a new character who, on the face of things, might be a little scary...but you'll see.

CHAPTER 5
RICKY BUDDY PLACE

One summer when Ricky was around twelve years old, he started taking off on his bike and staying gone all day. Now, let's get one thing straight. I had plenty to do, so I hardly noticed he was gone. Mom gave me breakfast first thing and a lot of days I'd chat with Murray for a while, and Tommy was good for a jaunt around the neighborhood, then Mom would kick into gear and do some errands, and if I stood there looking attentive and needy, she'd invite me to jump into the car and go with her. We'd stop over for short visits to friends, or go shopping around the town square, where I was always trotting alongside even into the shops. "Oh there's Ralph, he's such a handsome young man," would be the comment, or some such. When it came to the Supermarket, I had to stay in the car, but Mom always pulled under the trees on the north side of the parking lot and left the windows mostly open. Afraid I'd jump out or somebody would snatch me? No way. That didn't happen in our town.

At the beginning Mom would wave her finger at me and say, "Stay here Ralph and don't go anywhere." Of course, I didn't understand the words back then, but I could see what she meant and the meaning was clear. Most days, some man or woman would walk by, stick a hand through the open window and pet my head and say, "how you doin' today, Ralph." It was a nice town to live in.

So life was good, but the truth is, I kept wondering what Ricky was doing on his bike all day long. I paid careful attention around Mom to hear any hint of Ricky, but nothing came up, so one day when he peddled off down 4th Avenue, I followed him, far enough behind so I wouldn't be spotted. He took a left on Vine Street and a right on Tennessee Boulevard, crossed Main Street and into the circular driveway in front of Buddy's house. Ricky got off his bike and didn't look around, but I was a little more exposed than was comfortable, knowing that if he saw me, I'd be taken back home, so when he went inside, I called it a day and doubled back home to my yard.

For the next couple of days I tooled around town with Mom, but then I got the wild hair to follow Ricky again, and sure enough, he took the same route to Buddy's house. This time I stayed in the bushes on the North Tennessee Boulevard side next to the Fletcher's house. It was good cover in the low branches but I had to stay close to the ground because my coat is solid white from the neck down.

When they came out and jumped on their bikes, about fifteen minutes had passed. Riding on the sidewalks, they took a right on Cherry Lane and weaved over to Highland Avenue, and then straight for a while. It smelled differently over there than it did around my house, with mostly no sidewalks and the yards grew haphazardly to the edge of the street. I found it harder to stay undercover with no bushes near the street. Luckily the boys didn't look back as they were absorbed with lighthearted, playful chatter.

The air started to smell better and more like I was used to as we ambled out past open fields, until the bikes suddenly turned right into a field that stopped at a line of trees. While I smelled water, I couldn't see past the first few saplings.

After hanging around a while, I soon turned back to the road and headed home. Finding my way was easy, 'cause I remembered the smells and a few of the posts for the road signs. I saw a little yapping dog in a front yard and a cat up in a tree, but then, a big dog, let's call him Mr. Important, came off his front porch in an effort to defend his turf from me, the intrepid intruder, or so he thought. His lumbering gate and long ears bounded across the un-mowed grass, and I sensed a little fear in him, but mostly boredom as he raced toward me. I shot him the message that I was cool and just passing through, which he got, but too late to put on the brakes, so I stepped slightly to the left out of his path watching him screech by, finally resting in a pile at the bottom of a shallow drainage ditch. I shot him a cordial glance, put a little jump in my step, and continued home.

The next day I watched Ricky ride away, then took my time and trotted off through town and along the familiar trail to the new place. Two bikes lay on the leaves at the tree line when I arrived, and I strolled by them down to the creek to see the boys standing on small shallow rocks in the middle of a lackluster flow of clear water. The air cooled with each step that took me closer to the creek, and the bright summer sun faded to gray under that canopy of trees.

I found a hiding place and watched as they tooled around, just before Ricky said, "Hi Ralph." He wasn't surprised and didn't seem to care that I was there, then picked up a few small rocks and flung them into the creek while Buddy was stacking rocks up in a haphazard structure. Then I felt a presence. It was not fearful or dangerous, but it was strange and different. I stayed quiet, still in my hiding place.

An old man suddenly appeared without a sound, like he walked on air... he was so quiet. The boys were startled, but stood still and just looked up. Ricky held on to the few rocks he had not thrown and Buddy stopped and flashed his usual toothy smile. "Hi, I'm Buddy. And this is Ricky. This is our fort," he said.

"Just call me Zeke. And I guess it's kinda my fort too," the man said.

There was a long pause before Ricky asked, "Do you live here?"

"I guess I do. I have a small house a little bit up the creek." Zeke said.

"Can we see it?" Ricky asked.

"I guess so if you want to," Zeke said.

With no more than a nod, the boys followed the man up the creek a little bit, then ten feet up the bank, to a rough looking structure made out of scrap plywood. It was built into a small rock crevice that sheltered it from view. The man had to bend over to get into it, but when he came out he was holding a big seashell.

"Wow that's neat," Ricky said. "Where did you get it?"

"It's from the Pacific Ocean," Zeke said. "It's called a conch."

Then he raised the small end of the shell to his mouth and blew into it. The sound of a deep horn came out, and it scared me a little bit. After all, I'm a dog and sudden sounds scare me. At least that's what Mom told the boys one time.

Ricky picked up a stick and threw it at an old oak tree, then flung a hand-sized rock into the creek. Buddy walked up the creek a few steps surveying the the water's path and then asked Zeke, "Where do you come from?"

Zeke clasped his hands together level with his waist, then looked up and said, "Sorta nearby."

Ricky said, "Nashville?"

"Not that far," he said.

"I'll race you to the bikes," Buddy suddenly said.

"Bye Zeke," Ricky said. "Come on Ralph."

But I was half way up the hill by that time.

I'll confess that I got on high alert when Zeke first came up. I thought about my attack plan to protect the boys, but frankly it never felt like Zeke was a threat. Anyway, I think my bark might be worse than my bite, if you know what I mean.

Buddy picked his bike up by the handle bars and looked over at Ricky and me, "My Mom told me about Zeke. Everybody knows him cause he used to work in the shoe store on the square. He ran errands for my granddad at our store for awhile. He's a second cousin of officer Lester Jakes. Mom said he's not quite right, but if you leave him alone, he'll leave you alone."

I thought about, "What does 'not quite right' mean?" Buddy looked over at me and said, "It means you're not with it."

And what does "you're not ...?" Oh, never mind, I thought.

THERE'S MORE to come with Zeke, and to be honest, I'd say that I kinda like Zeke, but I'm in charge of security and can't afford to let down my guard. So I'll just say, Zeke presented no present danger. It sounds pretty cool, so I'll leave it at that.

GOSH, I really like these summer adventures. In the late 1950s, a small town didn't offer much entertainment or many distractions, and a popular thing to do was 'ride around.' Just jump in the car and wherever you started, you'd be on tattered blacktop and gravel roads in the country in a matter of minutes .

The best time to go was Sunday because the hay wagons and tractors were parked while church was going on. 'Riding around' made for a lot of cama- raderie, togetherness, and friendship building with young friends and also with families.

I liked to ride in the car with the windows open to smell it all, and I liked being with the family, so I was always ready to go when the car door opened. Come along on this fun story, 'cause I can't wait for you to meet Aunt Betty.

CHAPTER 6
AUNT BETTY

"Ralph, What's it like riding in a car?" Murray asked.

"What does it look like to you?" I said.

"Well it looks scary, but exciting too," he said. "You jump in that car almost every day, it seems. Do you get a stomach ache bumping up and down the road?"

"No way with Mom driving. Sometimes, though, Dad pops the boys and me into the car and we drive around the country roads, just looking at the fields, the cows, the barns, and the houses, and it can get bumpy. Sometimes Dad pulls up to somebody's house and we all get out and talk to the people Dad knows," I said.

"Is that called a farm?" Murray asked.

"I think it's a farm. Anyway, the smells are completely different. I mean the grass, and the bushes smell kind of minty," I said.

"What does 'minty' mean?" Murray asked.

"I'm not sure. I heard Ricky say it once," I said.

"Are there other dogs and cats on a farm?" Murray asked.

"Every farm has dogs and cats, cows and horses, There's a really nice Sheepdog at one of the farms who is golden-brown with a white collar and long legs, named Aunt Betty. She always runs up to me wagging her tail and gives me a little 'muzzle-bump.' She's really big and not scared of anybody. Good at conversation, too," I said.

"Does she like cows?" Murray asked.

"Well she didn't exactly say anything about cows, but she took me into the barn to see some of the stalls where horses stay at night," I said.

"What did that smell like?" Murray asked.

"The barn has mixed smells because the loft is full of hay which kinda smells like the outdoors, and when the big doors are open the wind from outside blows through," I said.

"Did you like it there?" Murray asked.

"You can roam around wherever you want and there are lots of moles and ground squirrels to chase and dig up...and not many cars," I said.

"Aunt Betty told me that one morning a small pack of dogs wandered onto her farm and tried to scare her by surrounding her, snarling and growling. She said before they knew what hit them, she made a quick lunge to the mouth of the lead dog opening up the side of his jaw and nose.

Then they made a circle around her, still growling until one dog lunged at her. She stepped aside and when it crashed into the dirt, Aunt Betty turned and ripped a gash in its neck. The others followed quickly as that one took off running, trailing a river of blood. I guess that pack still comes around, but keeps their distance from Aunt Betty."

"But she was really friendly to you, right?" Murray said.

"Yes she is friendly, but she knows how to take care of herself and her farm," I said.

"Do you know how to take care of yourself, Ralph?" Murray asked.

"I guess I do kinda. I'm not big like Aunt Betty, but I try to watch everything and be as smart as I can when bad things come up," I said.

I told him about Mr. Important racing at me and how I just stepped aside and let him crash into the ditch under his own momentum.

"Did you feel bad about that?" Murray asked.

"Not really," I said. "It's a dog-eat-dog world out there."

THE NEXT DAY AROUND MID-MORNING, Murray looked up and was watching the pearly-white puffy clouds amble by on top of a deep-blue summer sky. A gentle breeze blew a new scent my way from those little yellow blooms over by the garden, and I felt I needed to stroll over and scope out the action there. It was the same as yesterday, so after a few extra sniffs and a token marking, I sauntered back to the fence where Murray was sitting.

"Murray, do you know what a hobo is?" I asked.

"No clue. Where did you pick up that funny word?" He asked.

"Buddy was saying that the guy named Zeke, down by the creek, was called a hobo by some people."

"That's the guy with the horn?" Murray asked.

"Right. He has a good vibe and he already was talking to me in a nice way. Talk like we do, that is."

"Okay?" Murray said.

"He has the same clothes on every time I see him, and when he's around I can smell him right away," I said.

"Is it a bad smell?" Murray asked.

"I don't know what bad smells are because every smell just is what it is. I can tell how people feel or if there is a bit of sickness just by their smell. You know how your dad comes home some days after work and looks calm and happy, but is buzzing inside?"

"I think I do." Murray said.

"I can smell my dad's mood through his skin. Not only that, I can be in another room when he arrives and smell it immediately," I said.

"Do you try to tell your mom about your dad's mood?" Murray said.

"No, I rub up against his leg and when he sits down, I jump in his lap. After that I can tell the buzz starts to go away," I said.

"Cool," Murray said. "I'll ask my mom about that word, hobo."

"Do you talk to her much?" I asked.

"When we're all alone, it's quiet, and she's in the

right mood, I can ask things and she just thinks the answers right 'out loud to me.' Sometimes after we have had a nice conversation, she looks over at me and says, 'Oh Murray, you're so smart.'"

HEARING AUNT BETTY'S STORY, I learned a lot about myself and how the world we're in works. I get the impression that weak ones get picked on by the ones who can get away with it. Also, how weak or strong you are depends on what environment you find yourself in, and how your skills fit there. Aunt Betty didn't complain about it. She understood it, and knew her part. Country dogs seem to have a quiet, simple complacency. Sometimes I wonder if I'd like to live on a farm in the country.

Murray is my best friend, and things would be boring without him. But I'll be clear. He can have his moments. 'Moments' is what they say on TV when people do something weird. If you're wondering what I mean, move on to the next chapter, and I'll introduce you to Mister Weird and his friend, Lionsgate.

CHAPTER 7

MURRAY CHANGES HIS NAME

I jumped in the car with Tommy and Ricky as mom pulled out of the driveway onto 4th Avenue. She was headed to the elementary school on Lytle to drop Ricky off and then the two blocks to high school for Tommy.

"No Mom, I have to get there now. Right now!" Tommy blurted.

"It's just two blocks. It'll be fine," Mom responded calmly.

"I mean it. Take me first," Tommy repeated.

Mom turned left on Main Street instead of staying straight on Tennessee Boulevard, as she'd planned.

Tommy jumped out of the car without a word and started walking briskly toward the band room.

"Well, that got him here about two minutes early." Mom said to the air in the front seat of the car.

Ricky barely noticed the goings-on, and I just

watched from my back-seat perch, not saying a word.

~

WHEN WE PULLED into our driveway, I leaped out of the car from the driver's side and watched Mom disappear through the patio door. Time for my mid-morning security check of the yard. The fence separated us from 4th Avenue on one side and Murray's yard on the other, but didn't have a gate around the driveway. Mom told me how to look for cars when I first got here, so I look both ways and am careful.

At the far end of the fence there was some bird activity that needed my attention. When I got there, a blue jay was dive-bombing a couple of cardinals, or 'redbirds,' as we call them. Blue jays are bigger and use their size to get what they want. When a jay flew in, I barked loud enough to scare him away, then watched the redbirds fly back in and land on the dogwood tree. They gave me a wink and I knew my job was done. Birds don't talk much, so a wink is about all you can expect.

As I was heading back around to the driveway, I heard a familiar clunk on the fence.

"Hi Murray," I said in my top-of-the-morning-voice. "Did you see that jay over there? How mean is that?"

"Yeah, if that guy gets too close to me, I'll sink a claw into him and put an end to his fun," Murray replied.

I agreed but didn't say anything and just let it sit as a slight breeze twitched my ear.

Murray scratched around on the fence until he found a comfortable place.

"Ralph, I have an important announcement to make," he said with a serious tone in his voice.

"Let her rip," I said. "I'm all ears."

"I'm hereby changing my name."

"What? You can't just change your name. You're Murray. That's the name you were born with."

"Well I'm changing it. 'Murray' doesn't reflect who I am. I mean who I really am now, in this time, in this place. 'Murray' is mundane and normal. I'm much more than that," he said.

"Okay, how about we call you Uncle Buck?" I said.

"Very funny. Besides, that one's taken. Look Ralph, I'm a 'tortie' and I have special powers. I can bring good luck to an entire household," he said. "It's my heritage, my lineage and my obligation."

I looked up at a thin layer of autumn clouds gently rolling by. I was hoping for a spontaneous tornado, or random earthquake to get me out of this discussion without being rude. You know, a call-to-arms, some emergency barking. Anything.

"By rubbing my tail on a wart, people say it can cure an ugly blemish. I have special powers and I need a name that reflects that." Murray paused and then continued. "Male torties are very rare. I mean one in three thousand. Special, Ralph, think special.

Okay with no tornado in sight, I guessed I was in this thing.

"What is a tortie, Murray," I asked.

"It's a nickname for tortoiseshell. That's the color I am, brown and black and white all mixed in together," Murray said. "Some people in far-away places believe that torties were made from the blood of a young goddess."

Murray was staring out in space talking to the universe. He didn't notice the dead-pan look on my face or how I was just staring at the fence without the ability to say a word.

"What do you want to change it to?" I finally asked.

"Some people are quite sure that we torties can keep ghosts away from their house."

I stayed silent just sitting in the grass below the fence.

"I was thinking about Linus, or Lionel. A name that reflects a regal air. After all, lions are relatives of mine and they are king of the jungle," he said. "Maybe Lionsgate. That has a nice ring to it."

I was feeling my body going comatose, but in the most lethargic voice I could utter I said, "That's the name of a shopping center on the road to Nashville."

"What's a shopping center?" Murray asked.

"Okay Lionsgate, I see that blue jay again. Check you later," I said.

As I slinked away, I watched his regal-ness melding his soul with universal-truth in the deep recesses of who-knows-where.

≈

THERE'S NEVER a boring moment with Murray on the scene. We'll circle back on his name later. Now get ready for a wild ride with Zeke. He's going international with this intriguing story about an ocean voyage and a far away island. I'm not sure it's all really true...I think.

CHAPTER 8
CAPE HORN

Don't get me wrong; I like hanging out around the house and going on small car rides with Mom, but on Saturday, in the fall after school starts, the boys are around and it's more fun, especially since they run everywhere they go, and I get to pretend I'm chasing them. We live on a 'Place.' That's what you call a street that circles around and has a wide strip of land in the middle. There are trees on this center plot and a few bushes and the rest is grass. Some of the trees have low, strong limbs and not a lot of small branches. Those are for climbing. Tommy and Ricky climb those trees all the time, but Scott, the boy down the street, runs up and down them like he is a monkey. I saw monkeys climbing all over trees on a TV show. Scott swings and leaps from limb to limb, and all the kids call him a monkey and I guess he likes it, because he keeps laughing and swinging.

Tommy and I took off early one Saturday

morning and skipped on down to the Wilson's back-yard. They are building a little house in the back of their yard next to the fence, and Tommy wanted to check on the progress. None of the boards matched and although bigger, the outside looked like the house that fellow, Zeke, lives in. Early in the summer, the Wilson boys showed Tommy the hole in the fence where they'd crawl through to the new house being built and 'liberate' some of the 'extra' wood from the site. Tommy, with me by his side, squeezed through the fence and walked around, where I saw another new house and then another and another. Tommy said it was a subdivision. That's what you call it when they take a nice meadow that's perfectly good for running around and digging up field mice, and they build a lot of houses, and the people move in with loud kids and yippie little dogs. Yuk!

Later Tommy and I made our way back home, came through the side gate into our yard and walked around the house to the driveway, just in time to see Ricky 'round the corner and point his bike down 4th Avenue toward Buddy's house. Tommy headed inside through the back door, paused and looked at me.

"You coming in Ralph?" He asked.

I looked for a second and turned toward the fence and strolled away. Now I know that may seem a little rude, but I didn't want to go in and I can't exactly say it and a bark would be counter-produc-tive. Face it, it's the way dogs do it.

Heading down to Buddy's, I watched the cars for

a while before I decided to cross Main Street, just the way Mom showed me. When I rambled into his driveway, Ricky's bike was outside leaning against the steps. Buddy was never outside waiting; always a few minutes late. Pretty soon they bounded out and jumped on the bikes, headed up Main Street, a quick right onto Cherry Lane and off we went to the creek.

"Look at Ralph," Buddy said. "Where did he come from?"

"I don't know," Ricky replied.

The air was a little cooler now that summer was on the way out. It's kind of fun tramping down the street and wading through leaves everywhere. I asked Murray one time why the leaves fell off the trees.

"I think the trees get sick every year," he said. "Must be something they ate."

Murray is so smart; he knows everything.

THE BOYS TOOK the path from the edge of the field, weaving through the small stand of trees down to the creek and their fort, which consisted of rocks lining a small clearing. Buddy went right to work straightening them and adding new ones. Ricky had a small dam under construction to create a pool for wading and dipping your hands, or paws as I saw it. The water slid through, up and over the rocks in a neat pattern, but so far no pool had emerged.

Buddy pulled a small sack from his bike basket

and put it on a large root that circled up through the ground and back into the rocky soil, providing a nice lunch table. The bag settled in between the crags of knotty bark that had grown over the root to protect it from the weather. The sack held two sandwiches, one peanut butter and grape jelly, and the other a thin slice of cheese on Wonder Bread with a layer of mayonnaise and two bottles of RC Cola. It was a royal banquet if I ever saw one.

Nobody said much while the boys worked diligently on their projects. My main job was to sniff out any activity in and around the fort complex. I was chief of security and although I had no hot karate chops to combat intruders, I had a nose for trouble, so-to-speak. Often my investigations included digging into ant hills and ground-squirrel holes, and while this was the most urgent task I had, from time-to-time, I picked up signs of subtle activity. That day I detected people footprints on the right bank next to Ricky's dam, I looked up and over at the boys. I felt like they should be concerned at this discovery, before realizing that they did not or could not smell the intruder. I barked and waited for a look back so I could point out this important find, but they were lost in the tasks at hand.

After a break for lunch, I trotted up the path to check on the bikes. Emerging from the shaded tree line, the sun beat down on my white, short fur. I laid on the grass next to Ricky's bike for a few minutes and let the sun bake me till I was 'over-easy,' then headed back to the creek. As I entered the tree line I could smell trouble. The boys were busy as bees, when I saw him quietly walking down the middle of the creek, skipping from rock to rock, feet staying just above the water flow.

I heard a sound, so low that I knew the boys didn't hear it, but for me it cracked loud in my ear. A red-alert flashed in my mind, so I let go a series of barks. Buddy looked up to see Zeke approaching the fort.

"Hi Mr. Zeke," Buddy said.

"Good morning gentlemen," Zeke replied.

Buddy did small talk with Zeke, while Ricky worked on his dam project. I watched Zeke carefully for any sign that I would have to shift into attack mode and leap for the jugular. Okay, I can't really jump that high, but you know what I mean. I'm not an attack dog, but I am a dog and people stop what they're doing and look around when they hear a dog barking. Their neck might be safe, but nobody is happy with bloody knee caps, which is just what I'd have in mind.

I knew Zeke was okay, but I looked him over for good measure. I didn't sense any fear or danger in Zeke, and the funny thing is, his vibe was more like the boys than like Dad or Mom. He didn't laugh, but it felt like he was continually on the verge of laughing, or telling a joke, or smiling, not like the other grownups.

"Blow that horn of yours," Ricky said from his squatted perch overlooking the dam.

"Ah yes, the conch shell," Zeke said as he shifted back on his heels.

"Yeah, blow it again," Ricky reiterated.

"Where did you get that shell?" Buddy asked.

"Well," Zeke paused. "That's a long story. Do you boys like stories?"

"Sure we like stories," Buddy said looking at Ricky nodding his head.

~

"ONCE UPON A TIME, I was on the *Amelia Rose* headed around the Cape on route to the Pacific Ocean," Zeke said.

"What's a cape?" Ricky asked.

"Cape Horn, my little man," Zeke replied. "It's land that sticks out into the ocean at the bottom of the world. It's the roughest, ugliest, most dangerous sailing on the planet. Captain Jonas was taking a load of clothing, farm equipment, and some other things, all made in the eastern states down around the Cape to San Francisco. The boat was named for the captain's wife, he claimed for good luck."

"Is that where you got the shell?" Buddy asked.

"Sit tight big boy. There's more to this story," Zeke said. "Cape Horn is the dividing line between the Atlantic and the Pacific Oceans. The winds and the sea churn from all directions and our passage was like walking on a razor's edge, it was so scary. I thought we were all going to drown. Somehow we made it through to the mighty Pacific. We rounded the Horn and started north to California when about two days out, a big storm hit, and it was the worst thing ever. We suffered two weeks of driving rain, and the wind never let up."

"Did you all die?" Buddy said.

"Of course they didn't die, or he wouldn't be here," Ricky injected.

"Did everybody die but you?" Buddy persisted.

"We were blown off course straight west, and when the storm moved past us, *Amelia Rose* was barely floating, but the captain found a small group of islands to rest and repair the boat. And nobody drowned, we all made it."

"Did you get the shell there?" Ricky asked.

"Yes the shell came from the Marquesas' Islands. It took a month to fix the boat and I had nothing to do, so I hiked all over the island."

I wanted to ask Zeke an important question, so I thought real hard and concentrated on Ricky in hopes he'd 'hear' me. He looked my way and gave me a little grin.

Then Ricky's eyes trained on Zeke and said, "Do they have dogs there?"

"A few." Zeke replied and then said, "After a while, I hiked over the mountains and found villages of people that lived away from everybody, a place with almost no roads. The people were very friendly, and they gave me a place to sleep and meals of fruit, vegetables, and fish."

"Did you want to stay there and live forever?" Buddy asked.

"Well, it's funny you should ask that. I met a girl there and fell in love."

"Is she your wife?" Buddy asked.

"She was when I was there, but the captain sent two sailors over the mountains to bring me back to the boat. I told her I would go with them to tell the captain that I wasn't going back with him. She gave me the conch shell and I promised to return."

"Wow!" Ricky said.

"As soon as I walked on the boat, the captain threw me in a room and locked the door, only letting me out after two days that took us a hundred miles away."

"Did you ever go back to the island and get your wife?" Buddy asked.

"That's a sad question, my young friend," Zeke replied. I sent letters for a long time, but never got a reply, and finally realized, that village doesn't get mail. If someone leaves, they're gone. If they return, they're back. It's that simple."

Zeke paused, and the boys didn't say a word.

Then he said, "I tried to save up the money to go back, but I never could."

I watched Zeke and could feel his anxiety and disappointment, and the pain in his heart. When I tried to look away, his burning eyes held my stare. I thought about my first September with the family when Ricky and Tommy went to school, and it was so quiet. At first I thought they'd never come back. That's when I felt that same feeling of anxiety and disappointment for the first time.

Then Ricky said, "Hey Zeke, can you help me with my dam?"

Zeke's smile returned and the spell holding me broke as he stepped over to the little rock pile Ricky had assembled.

A while later we packed up and I followed the

boys home thinking about Zeke, the beautiful island, and the beautiful girl.

I ALMOST FELT like I was on the Amelia Rose for that trip around the bottom of the world. With that kind of adventure and danger, Zeke is lucky to be home safe, and perched down by the creek. Read on to the next chapter for the new twist Murray has for you... he's tired of living. Really! You're going to love this story. As they say, 'You can't make this stuff up.'

CHAPTER 9
A FULL LIFE

"Ralph, I'm not sure I want to keep living," Murray quietly said one morning when I was strolling across the yard.

Looking up I saw Murray, as expected, on the fence in front of a background of waning bougainvillea plants loosing leaves and sketching out a winter look of naked vines on the side of his house.

"What's this all about, Murray?" I asked.

Murray sighed and looked off in the distance of the neighborhood, past the electric polls strung in sequence with black lines as far as a cat-eye could see.

"I've had a full life. Done just about all a cat can accomplish in one lifetime."

"Oh yeah? Tell me about that," I said.

"Shepherded Mom through childbirth and practically raised Jimmy...got him through diapers—that was 'odoriss' if you know what I mean—into school,

and now he's in sixth grade. He's practically raised...
a virtual adult," Murray continued. "Well I wasn't
actually there during childbirth. That was during
Muffy's watch. But I've virtually eradicated the
mouse population over on my side of the fence, and
the few spiders still here know to steer clear of me,
old Lionel, himself," he said.

"Wait a minute, I thought your new name was
Lionsgate," I inserted.

"Don't be silly, that's a shopping center," he said
and whisked his glance toward the eastern skies.

Now, we all know that Murray's fur is the
weaved-in color of ginger-red, black, and white,
kinda-like the tortoise shell that he is so proud of. In
general, the parents of 'torties' know them as high
energy, sassy, and sometimes aggressive. Instead of
attitude they call it "tortitude." Murray takes it to a
new level, however. I wouldn't go so far as to actually call Murray weird, but the thought does cross
my mind at certain times...like this time.

"How were you planning to end-it-all, my furry
friend?" I asked.

"I don't know. Maybe throw myself under a
bus." He replied.

"That may be a problem," I said.

"Why? I'll just watch for the bus, leap under the
front tire, and then...then it'll be over...a life well
lived...lived to the fullest. What more can a cat ask
for?" Murray concluded with a sigh followed by a
whimper.

"For one thing, our town doesn't have buses any
more. They tried a few but nobody rode on them

because our town is too small and they didn't go many places and they never ran on time," I said. "You could throw yourself under a bike tire, but it might not kill you, just break a leg or two. Then everybody would say you're stupid or senile or both. You could end up being the laughing-stock of the whole town."

"What does senile mean?" Murray asked.

"I'll tell you in a few years when we get buses again," I said. "Let's go see what the blue jays are messing with down at the corner, and we'll talk about your future plans later."

"Okay. Those birds probably need some supervision anyway."

WHAT CAN I SAY. Another fun day in the asylum with Murray. Moving on, you'll get a laugh in this next chapter. Zeke made a comment that was just an aside. But that little snippet caught my attention, and when I mentioned it to Murray, the fun began.

CHAPTER 10
PENCILS HAVE ERASERS

Through the sliding glass door I could see the day brightening up, as well as a slight glimmer of sunshine reflecting off the outdoor grill's chrome handle. When I heard Mom rounding the corner from the hall, and heading into the den, I stood close to the door, looked up at her, and like clockwork, Mom stopped, grabbed the door handle and slid it open.

"Okay Ralph," she said. "Looks like it's warmed up enough. Go have fun."

Since Christmas the weather settled into a wintery January with overcast skies, and cold temperatures. Other than a couple of potty stops a day, I've stayed inside, so it was nice to take a stroll.

I didn't expect to see any real action, so thought I'd sniff around for ground squirrels or the dreaded moles that Dad hates; even the blue jays stay out of sight, and some of those guys fly down to Florida for the winter. One day I wasn't in the mood to chase them and I asked a fellow named Bonaire about it and he said some years he vacations in the south and others he just stays put. I guess he's a Jetsetter. Sounds a little uppity to me.

Anyway, I was looking up at the jay's corner-perch on the fence, when I heard the familiar clump sound.

Without looking around, I thought out loud, "Didn't expect you out here this morning. Thought you'd be sitting with Uncle Buck around the fire place."

"Yeah, well I snuck out the cat-door," Murray said. "What's new?"

"Nothing really, just killing time and waiting for Spring," I said.

"What do you do 'just killing time'?" Murray asked.

"I've been watching TV a lot. I like the 20-Mule-Team-Borax show. It's in the wild west, wherever that is. But I do know it's hot and dry, and everybody wears a big hat, and they all talk mean to each other, and somebody is always chasing somebody else. All five of us gather around the TV and they fight to see who gets to sit with me," I said. "But other times the last few months, I've been thinking about something that guy, Zeke, down at the creek said."

"Oh, that guy?" Murray said. "What did he say?"

He was telling the boys a story about fishing for Marlin off the Florida coast the time his boat sprung a leak."

"What's a Marlin?" Murray asked.

"It's a fish, don't interrupt," I said.

After the story, it was kind of quiet and Zeke said, "Nobody's perfect, that's why they put erasers on pencils."

Ricky said, "I like erasers," and Buddy said, "yeah, they're good."

But I've been thinking about that phrase lately.

"Is that the end of the pencil that I like to chew off?" Murray said.

"Yes that's how you destroy all pencils within your reach."

"Well then, Ricky and I have something in common. We both like erasers," Murray said.

"Murray, you are such a dork!"

"What's a dor...."

"Don't even go there," I said. "I'm talking about the bigger meaning. Nobody is perfect is like saying everybody makes mistakes. And erasers are there to correct mistakes. Do you get it?" I asked.

"So you think it's a mistake to chew the eraser end off the pencils?" Murray said.

"Murray, you are driving me mad," I yelled.

"Gotcha, my canine friend," he said. I know what a mistake is, and I've made my share of them. I'm glad we can have do-overs, and get it right. Sometimes even if you can't correct it, it doesn't turn out as bad as you thought it would."

Murray is so wise.

～

THERE'S SO MUCH in Murray's head, I'm surprised it doesn't explode. I think I'll tell him that if things aren't that bad, maybe the throwing-yourself-under-the-bus idea is not all that smart. Enough about Murray.

Next is a touching story about Ricky and Tommy. You'll notice that Ricky always wanted to do whatever Tommy was doing, like a second child does. Tommy takes the front seat in this story about growing up. You may be able to relate, if you're interested in growing up.

CHAPTER II

ON THE SPORTS FIELD

"Come on Ralph," Ricky yelled across the driveway. "Dad's ready to leave."

I put a little bit of giddy-up in my step, ran across the yard, and leaped into the back seat with Ricky. Tommy was in the front next to Dad driving. Dad came home early and we were going to the high school sports field to watch football practice. He wanted to show Tommy what practice was all about in case he had any thoughts about playing himself. Ricky was beaming with excitement because he was hanging with his two favorite guys —well three including me.

Turning off Main Street, we weaved through the parking lot and pulled up to the chain-length fence. A few dads were watching their sons running up and down, starting and stopping, and banging into each other. I could feel the "dad vibrations." Some of them were excited, and some felt like they were young again and on the field themselves. Some felt trepidation and a bit of fear that their son wouldn't make the grade and get kicked off the team. But one thing for sure, there was a thrill in the air.

Wintertime was fading, and a warm afternoon sun was beginning to coax the jonquils out of the ground along the fence line. They came up every spring from bulbs lying dormant through the winter, with small little yellow buttercup blossoms that smelled like pure honey to me.

Loosing interest in young boys sweating and grunting, I followed my nose along the fence looking for fledgling dandelions to root up. I could almost taste the sweet scent of these youngster plants poking through the dirt to start a new and exciting life. But I dug them up anyway. You know that thing where dogs dig with their front paws tossing the dirt back in a frantic fit, then intently dragging their back paws over the ground like on a door mat? You got it. I'm a dog. That's the way we do it.

Circling back around, I walked up to Dad and Tommy.

"Well, what do you think?" Dad said to Tommy.

"It's cool, Dad. Football is cool." He replied.

Tommy wasn't small for his age, but he wasn't a big boy. He liked touch football in the circle in front of our house. In fact, I liked it too, although I learned to pay attention and stay out of the way. At first I just chased the boys up and down, running along beside them, but Van Wilson was older, and while doing a lot of the running with the ball, he would kick me out of the way and sometimes step on me. I yelped with pain and looked up to Tommy for some sympathy, but I got none. They were all scrambling and running and I learned quickly and painfully that the sidelines were the best place for me. It was a good lesson. I guess we all need lessons.

"What do you think?" Dad said. "Those guys have to work hard and toughen up. We could get some weights and put together a little gym in the garage. What do you think big man?"

Tommy stood at the fence with a straight back holding his head up, exuding confidence and poise. Then I felt something in the breeze when he glanced over at me and in my mind's eye I could see parts of a model train all over the garage, and I could feel how engaged he was with it. Tommy liked figuring things out and putting them together. He was going to fill that garage up all right, but not with weights. Tommy didn't exactly know it, but he was going to be an engineer. I just had that sense.

"Hey Dad, I like football," Ricky said as he inched over to Dad.

"Great, Ricky. What's your favorite thing? Running, catching, passing?" Dad asked. "Do you play at school on your field?"

"Yep we play at 10:30 recess. I don't get to play much. They always pick me last and nobody gives me the ball. But I watch 'em, and I chase whoever has the ball. It's fun running around," he said.

Dad's goal was Tommy that day, so he let that slide.

Then that breeze blew again right into my eyes and I could see as clear as a bell. Ricky was not going to be playing football, he was bound for things he could tackle within himself, like an artist or writer. He had a different kind of passion and vision than was suitable for football or really sports in general. Oh yeah, and he was way too small. But of course, in my case I think small is good. I don't know how I knew that stuff, but I was sure I was right.

"Cool Dad. Maybe we can talk about football later," Tommy said in a cheerful voice.

"Okay, maybe we will," Dad said.

TRYING to tell that story to Murray was futile. I never got past the buttercups. The next tale that Zeke told the boys was as good as before...or maybe better. Anyway, it covered a lot of ground from Spain to the Everglades. From Spanish gold and silver coins to alligators. Great fun!

CHAPTER 12
THE BIG ONES EAT THE LITTLE ONES

"A wrong turn can be the right thing sometimes. That's what he said when we were sitting around Zeke's enormous campfire," I explained.

"How big was the fire?" Murray asked.

"I guess regular size as fires go, but it was warm and seemed big to me," I said.

"'Cause you're a runt compared to people," Murray said with a smirk.

"Yeah, tell me about it Mr. Lionsgate," I said.

"That's Lionel to you, Mr. Watchdog," he said.

Sometimes Murray could be in a sassy mood, and today was one of those days. I took a slight stroll around the flower garden and ended up back at the fence with Murray staring down at me.

"Zeke told us a story about getting on a wrong boat and ending up in Spain and then later in Central America when he meant to board a boat to New York Harbor where there was a job on the docks waiting for him. He was late and running for the boat, stopped to ask a dock worker which boat went to New York. The guy thought for a minute and said Oceana Iberia with the dark blue hull. So Zeke ran and jumped on the ramp where he was the last man to get on," I said.

"Is this Zeke guy for real?" Murray asked.

"Look he has his own house and his own fire; he must be," I said. "Anyway they pulled out of the harbor and Zeke showed them his ticket. That's when he found out he was going to Spain," I said.

"Did the guy on the dock lie to him?" Murray asked.

"He doesn't think so. The boat he should have taken to New York was the Oceana Bull," I said. "Anyway he landed in Castile, Spain at a time when loads of gold and silver coins were being shipped over from Central America. They paid him in gold coins for working on the dock, and after a year he jumped on a boat to the Caribbean Islands."

"What are coins?" Murray asked.

"Little round things people use to buy all the stuff they want." I said.

"Why do they want stuff?" he asked.

"Well, stuff like cat food," I said.

"Okay then. I get it," Murray said. "Did some pirates make him walk the plank and get eaten by a big whale?"

I stopped and cleared my throat...well you know, not really but I swallowed and then said, "Murray have you been watching movies again on T.V.?"

"All the guys on that show I watched were

tough, had long hair, bandanas around their heads, and were poking each other with big, shiny sticks," he said. "Do we have pirates around here?"

"Of course not. All that happened hundreds of years ago. Everybody now days is honest, well except maybe politicians'" I said.

"What's a poll-i-ti-tan?" Murray said.

"They're the men who live in big red-brick buildings and smoke cigars," I said. "And by the way, those sticks are called swords. They're sharp and are made to cut peoples' heads off."

"Did that character, Zeke, get his head cut off?" Murray said.

Murray was being difficult 'cause I was sure he knew better than that. I stood up and started to walk over to chat with the two blue jays that landed on our fence, when I heard him screech out, "Just kidding, but seriously is Zeke, like two hundred years old?"

"I don't know how old any people are. I don't even know how old I am," I said. "But sometimes I get the idea that Zeke is embellishing his stories."

"Okay Mr. Bookends, what does that mean," Murray said.

"He makes some of it up."

"Do Ricky and Buddy believe all his stories?" Murray asked.

"Yes I think so."

We both let that sit for half a minute before I continued with the story.

"He said that his job was to count the gold coins and write down the numbers and one day a big chest of gold just showed up at his door and nobody was around. He waited a few days to see who came for it and when nobody did, he bought a big boat, sailed it to Florida and never had to work again."

"That's why he has his own house and his own fire?" Murray said.

"I guess so," I replied. "I suppose getting on the wrong boat was the best thing that ever happened to him."

MURRAY JUMPED off the fence and disappeared into his yard. The sun was high so I saw no reason to make any sudden moves. Falling into a summertime snooze, I dreamed about piles of golden coins and plopping myself down onto a silky cloud of wealth and privilege. That's when I heard the plunk of Murray landing on the fence.

"That Zeke guy is a real piece of work," he blurted. "I wonder what else he has up his sleeve?"

"Did I tell you about after he landed in Florida?" I asked.

"Okay, I'll bite. What happened?" he said.

"Do you know what an Everglade is?" I said.

"It's air spray, right? Everybody knows that's the stuff your mom sprays into the room to make it smell like your dad didn't just walk out of the bath-room," Murray said.

"No Murray, it's a place full of water and alliga-tors, fish, and birds. All kinds of stuff."

"Did you say alley cats? And do they have dogs there?" Murray replied.

Sometimes talking to Murray was...well you know, difficult. But we've been through that.

"No, they're alligators and they're like lizards except bigger," I said.

"I like lizards," he said. "When I lie still, lizards sometimes run by me without noticing and I like it when they stop to look around. That's when I nab them. One quick paw on their back with claws out and I can bat them back and forth for an hour or as long as they last. But it's not much fun anymore, seems like I've whittled down the population in my yard."

"I looked up alligators in the dictionary when I was researching the Everglades," I said. "Trust me, you aren't going to be batting around any alligators. Big ones are eight feet long and weigh two hundred pounds."

"Is that big?" he said.

I ignored him for sanity reasons, then said, "Zeke told us that the ocean backs up and fills the low lands with salt water then the rivers dump fresh water into the Everglades when the big rains fall in summer. Alligators stay away from salt water, but like fresh water, so they only live in the Everglades in summertime."

"Zeke got a job running boats for fishermen and hunters who like to eat the fish and take the alligators home," I said.

"Do the alligators live in their yards after that?" Murray asked.

"Zeke said that they only take the skin home and make shoes and belts and furniture out of it," I said.

"Is that mean, treating animals like that?" he asked.

"Zeke said it's part of the food chain. The big ones eat the little ones. He said the alligators eat the raccoons, but get this, when the alligators are young, the raccoons just grab them and eat them like people eat chicken legs," I said.

"So the big alligators eat the raccoons that got big by eating the little alligators?" Murray said.

"The big ones eat the little ones," I said.

Then he said, "Wow, that Zeke is really smart."

Okay, Zeke might be making some of this up, but I'm never going to really know for sure, because I'm just a dog. Next meet my friend, Woody. He gets into a little trouble and you'll be surprised who comes off the fence to help out.

CHAPTER 13

WOODPECKER

There's a friend of mine we call, Woody. You guessed it; he's a woodpecker. Woody likes our neighborhood because there are a lot of trees that insects like and Woody is an expert at extracting them from the bark and slurping them up. He is also partial to several backyards that keep bird feeders stocked up all winter.

Mom thought Woody was a Yellow-Bellied Sapsucker and her nickname for him was Little Yellow. Last winter when Ricky was doing a school project on birds, I was snuggled next to him reading along when I saw a picture of Woody (aka Little Yellow). Ricky was about to turn the page so I inched my nose onto the book long enough to finish reading the description. I found out that Yellow-Bellied Sapsuckers look a lot like Woodpeckers. They fly south for the winter, while Woody is always waiting out the cold days here in the neighborhood.

Ricky reached for the corner of the page again,

but I gave him a subtle high-pitched 'dog noise' that focused him back on the picture of Woody.

"Wow, Ralph, that one looks like our little bird. I'm going to show Mom. I bet he's a woodpecker," Ricky said to my great satisfaction.

Woody was what you might call fickle in that he flitted around the neighborhood, so you never could count on him stopping by at any particular time. He was not audacious or flamboyant, but you always knew when he was around, because he liked to 'drum' on the gutter pipes, or a board on the fence that made a deep, resonant sound that he liked.

"What's that rat-tat-tat noise?" Dad asked one time while he and Mom were sitting on the patio.

Mom looked up and said, "That bird, Ricky's woodpecker, is marking his territory."

"Could he mark it on someone else's gutters," Dad said.

"No dear, he likes your gutters," she replied.

WOODY ALSO LETS GO a sharp chirp before landing on a feeder or tree limb, which notifies me when he's visiting my yard. One day when the air was still cold, and the new leaves had only barely started to peek out from the bare branches, I heard the familiar chirp. I turned my head to see Woody on a slow dive to the feeder just outside our kitchen window. Right then, I heard a sound like a freight train and watched a freak gust of wind surge from behind, tumble Woody head over heels and slam him into the window.

I held my ground and looked for him to pull himself up and regroup, but nothing moved as the loud gust dissipated to quiet stillness. Then a blue jay swooped in and did a pass at Woody, pecking him sharply. Woody still didn't move. I saw the jay round out and line up for another strike, when I jumped up and threw myself between the villain and the woodpecker. Normally my barking would have brought Mom and the boys outside, but they had all gone to the grocery store; I was on my own. That is until I saw a figure dart past the patio table.

"Murray! What are you doing here," I said. "You almost never leave your yard."

"I thought those jays might gang up on you, and you might need added firepower," he said.

"You're helping a bird?" I asked. "I thought you like to eat birds."

"I talk a big game and every now and then I do eat one, but Woody is one of the good guys in the neighborhood, so I'm standing up for him. Besides I'd like nothing better than to dig my claws into that cocky jay and pull him down to my side of reality. Then we'll see who likes to eat birds."

Murray positioned himself directly in front of the site and along with my barking, the jay stayed clear. Some time passed and finally Woody's eyes slowly opened. He startled a bit when he saw Murray, but immediately got the picture. Right before Mom returned with the groceries, Woody flew up to a maple tree limb, rested for a moment and then disappeared.

"I'm headed for a nap by the fire," Murray said.

"Good idea, partner," I replied.

A couple of days later Woody landed on the fence next to Murray and thanked us for our help.

"I stayed out of sight for a few days cause it's hard to fly being dizzy," Woody said.

We nodded in agreement and the three of us sat in quiet relaxation.

Then out of the blue, Murray said, "How do you learn to fly?"

My lip was buttoned tight while Woody shot me an inquisitive glance and then said, "I don't know how to fly, and I don't know how not to fly. I'm a bird, Murray. It just comes naturally."

Murray's head turned to the side while I slowly rose to my feet and pointed myself toward the patio. You can't beat Murray to keep things strange.

WHILE WE'RE all waiting for Murray to learn to fly, I'll introduce you to an important life lesson in the next chapter. There's skating around a parking lot with milkshakes and cheeseburgers in this one. But, it's not about that. It's about being humble. But of course, it's a lesson delivered in 'Murray style.' Turn the page, the fun is waiting.

CHAPTER 14
DON'T GET ABOVE YOUR RAISIN

"You look bored, Ralph," Murray said one afternoon when I was lying in the warm sun, belly exposed to old Sol himself...that's what Dad sometimes calls the sun, Sol.

"Well Murray, it's good to know you haven't degraded your imagination, but what in the name of Sam Peet do you mean by that?" I said.

"Maybe you're not bored, but I'm tired of everything, like listening to my mom and dad going on all last night about all these old guys they knew," Murray said.

"What old guys?" I said.

"They were all over Uncle Buck last night, like what he used to say that made them fall over laughing, and then some of the trouble he'd get into," he said.

Now, in my older age and growing maturity level I know a few things about being a friend, although it's mostly being a therapist when Murray's

69

involved. So I sat in the sun and let him go on and on. Honestly, it broke up the afternoon and if I played it right it might keep me occupied until dinnertime.

"Good old Uncle Buck," I said. "Is he still occupying the mantle at chez Belchors?" I said.

"Yep, he's staying pretty quiet in his urn." Murray said.

"Does he ever talk to Muffy?" I asked.

"Not in front of me. I don't think he's hanging around the house. Maybe he is not as fond of the family as they are of him," Murray replied. "Or maybe he stays on the other side of the veil mucking around and getting into trouble."

Okay then. This was a little too far off the reservation for me, but being a listener, I let him talk. Building up anxiety and resentment is bad for anybody's health and sometimes after talking it through that stuff will simply fly out of your brain and leave you peace. Except in Murray's case it rarely flies, but moves more like a slow laborious crawl...oozing out through his ears into droplets of shear leftover madness. But then, I exaggerate.

"Listen to this one about Uncle Buck's first job. He was a waiter on roller skates at the Steak and Shake in Cincinnati," Murray continued.

"That's a whole different town, somewhere pretty far away," I said. "How did he get there?"

"I don't know where it is, but Uncle Buck couldn't find any work around here so he hitched a ride up there and tried to get a job in the tire factory, but he didn't get hired so he went looking around.

Finally ending up at this burger place, he asked the guy for a job," Murray said.

Okay, so right about then I was getting really bored and was thinking I'd head inside and see what was on T.V.

"The guy asked him if he could skate," Murray said. "Hey Ralph, what does it mean to skate, anyway?"

"You strap wheels on your feet and roll around," I said.

"How can you stand up with wheels on your feet?" Murray asked.

"You can't, Murray. It's for people," I replied.

"Well apparently it wasn't for Uncle Buck either," he said. He strapped on those skates and started rolling around the parking lot delivering milkshakes, cheeseburgers, and Cokes."

"Did he serve fries too?" I asked.

"What's a fry?" Murray asked.

"Never mind. Go on."

"His first customer rolled down the window just as Uncle Buck skated up next to the car with food on a tray. A little piece of gravel on the pavement stopped the wheels from rolling on his right foot, but didn't stop his hands and the tray from tipping and cascading through the open window onto the customer," Murray said. "Uncle Buck could see the food flying out of control, and reached out to catch what he could, but instead his hand batted the sixteen ounce Coke over the driver's head and onto the cute little girl in the passenger seat. The lid of the Coke hurdled off in flight and the whole thing gushed onto the perfect hairdo of the girl."

"What was Uncle Buck's next job?" I asked.

"It's worse than that," Murray said. "The manager must have anticipated a natural learning curve, so the waiters on wheels had to pay for the food as they picked it up, and then collect from the customer when it was delivered."

"So how did he make money?" I asked.

"He lost money," Murray said. "His next job was going back home."

"You're right. Uncle Buck was a colorful character," I said fearing he would rev up another story. The luckiest thing all day, was right then Mom called me for dinner.

∼

I FINISHED a hearty meal of dried food and leftovers, and Mom let me out again. To my surprise there was Murray on the fence. I figured things were safe because he got the Uncle Buck story off his chest.

"Ralph can you guess one of Uncle Buck's favorite sayings?" Murray asked.

I thought for a minute with no earthly idea of an answer and tried for the life of me to come up with something clever to move the conversation along, but in my silence Murray continued.

"Don't get above your raisin. That is it, all of it. At first I didn't get it but now it's clear," he said.

I stood firm in my 'listener' mode and didn't say a word.

"When Mom drops a raisin on the floor, I used to dart over and scarf it up, then over to my scratching platform to chew on it. But I was missing all the fun. You see the raisin just sits there and waits for me to slowly pick it apart, and believe me it's tedious, all shriveled up and a funny smell. It's too easy and drains the excitement out of the whole thing," he said to my utter amazement.

"So now after thinking over Uncle Buck's saying, I crouch down and stay low, batting it back and forth between my paws. I never standup and get above my raisin, which enables me to push it straight over to the platform or take my time and slide it around the kitchen floor. It's like a live event and it's a lot more fun. 'Don't get above your raisin.' That Uncle Buck sure was a smart guy," he said.

Now you may imagine how I was feeling right about then, not knowing whether to laugh or find a bomb shelter to hide in. Then I thought of the unthinkable. What if Murray could vote? Nah, forget it. He's a cat and even if they let cats vote, he would never pass the mental competency test.

Should I have mentioned that "don't get above your raising" means don't get uppity and think you're better than everybody else; respect the way you were brought up. It has nothing to do with a shriveled up grape they call a raisin. I gave a slight nod to Murray and turned toward the back door with my back straight and a confident pace, just like I was raised.

"I hear my TV calling," I said turning my head toward the fence.

"How does a TV call you?" Murray asked.

"I'm done here," I said.

Murray paused and then said, "If you're done, you're in the oven. You're either finished or through."

"Good night, Murray."

I THINK Murray is like a TV program that's really exciting, but after a while you need a break. In the South, the name for a special character is, 'a piece of work.' Murray checks all the boxes for that title.

I want to apologize, right up front, for the next chapter. It may look like I'm showing off my reading skills, but I'll take the hit just so I can share the Uncle Art letters. I'm not going to tell you which one is my favorite, but if you guess something about Roger, I won't be able to deny it.

CHAPTER 15

UNCLE ART LETTERS

Last Tuesday Mom raced out the door into the morning rain to take the boys to school, but when she didn't come back, I found myself stuck in the house in what felt like forever. I nosed around the bedrooms. Tommy had a book open on his desk that I paged through. I could read it, but I didn't know what most of the words meant. There were funny squiggly lines and some numbers. Then I wandered into Ricky's room and thumbed through a few pages of *Huckleberry Finn* from where we left off last night. I like the river and chasing around in the woods that's in that book.

Strolling into the kitchen to visit my water bowl for a drink, I saw the scrapbook Mom was working on, and hopped up on the chair to look it over. Hand written on the inside cover was, 'Uncle Art's Letters.' Every now and then Mom takes a small stack of letters and pastes them into the book. I figured

Huckleberry and the river would wait for awhile, so I read the first letter.

'HI MEG, It's Uncle Art. Well to start off, we're fine, even though the whole world is coming apart at the seams. Just read the papers. It's all terrible. Your cousin, Roger, is being real difficult and your great Aunt Beatrice put herself to bed a week ago and won't get up. It's worse than that, though. We had Sunday dinner for the whole family last week, and your third cousin, Billy Bob, took Roger's new sports car for a joy ride and busted a headlight. Billy Bob said he didn't do it, but was caught red-handed in a lie. Then Billy Bob said some people don't have to tell the truth and he was one of them. Roger got up on that old stump in the front yard and started railing against politicians and bankers and how they lie all the time. Aunt Beatrice watched the whole thing from a prone position through her window. I don't suspect we'll see her outside her room anytime soon.

Other than that, things are pretty normal around here. Come out to see us sometime and bring Andrew and the boys, and throw in that little scrawny dog, Rowland, too. They took the bridge out over the creek after the flood washed away the road, so you'll have to come around the long way through Silas Fester's farm. It's okay now 'cause they made him take the gate down and stop charging every car $1.50 to get by. His wife's got the gout, but I'll tell you about that another time.

Love, Uncle Art.'

∼

I LET OUT a loud bark and would have said a curse word if I could talk. What does he mean scrawny? Rowland? Rowland is a name for a sassy little poodle or some other foo-foo breed. I need to go out to the country and show Uncle Art just what a real, manly dog looks like. One named Ralph.

But then I sat back in the chair and took a minute to think about it. Maybe it was an honest mistake, although I'm a dog and don't really know what that means, but Mom says it all the time especially about people in the church who do dumb things. I think it means that he didn't intend to hurt my feelings or call me a poodle. I actually like the poodle across the street. His name is Pupin and he can run really fast. He doesn't talk much but that's okay.

When we go out there, I think I'll cut Uncle Art a break and not hold a grudge. I guess I'm a city dog and Ralph is a more sophisticated name than any old country-hick mama's-boy poodle anyway. I jumped down for a drink and then leaped back up on the chair to review another letter.

∼

'Hi Meg, It's Uncle Art. First of all Merry Christmas. I wanted to drop you a quick letter to thank you for the Sears Catalogue. I know it'll come in handy for Christmas shopping as we don't get into town much these days. Norma died on November 21, her funeral was December 12. This was Billy Ray's wife, 94, they cremated her. Shirley is busy cooking something for lunch and also for Christmas and Uncle Buford has an appointment in Nashville for his sinuses, out-patient.

Till next time, Uncle Art.

~

I heard the car door slam and knew Mom was finally home. Jumping off the chair, I made a B-line to the back door. The door swung open.

"Ralph, how did you get along while I was gone?" she asked.

Oh fine, I said.

~

I would like to ride in Roger's new sports car, the one with the new headlight, next time we head to the country. Hopefully I can avoid Aunt Beatrice.

A musical treat awaits you in the next chapter, or you might think it's a dancing 'train wreck.' Either way, I was dragged into it, so it's not my fault. Read along and see if you can swing with the beat.

CHAPTER 16

THE TWIST

Mid-morning in June was usually sunny and cool, or as people say it, 'not too hot yet.' I had breakfast when the boys got up and took my lap around the outer perimeter, or the "fence-line" for you regular people. Mom had been racing between the washing machine and the vacuum cleaner all morning while I found a nice perch in front of the couch watching the soap operas. 'Days of Our Lives' was my favorite, but when it was over, just watching Mom scurry around was wearing me out. As usual in this circumstance, I peddled over to the sliding glass door and stood. Not being in any great hurry, I didn't bother throwing Mom a suggestion to speed thing up. Then her steps slowed as she reached over me and opened the door. I tossed her a 'thank you,' and as I crossed the threshold onto the patio she said, 'you're welcome.' Mom and I really have things all nailed down.

A couple of robins and a finch were grazing for worms in the yard, but took a quick look at me and retreated to the maple tree that hung over from Murray's yard. I looked outside the fence at 4th Avenue from the end of our driveway seeing one car shuffle by, and a bicycler a few block away. Before I even got to the street, I could smell the mark of that neighborhood menace, Branford. He lives two whole blocks away, but revels in marking the ground right outside my driveway. I warned him not to keep doing that, and you know what he said? 'What are you going to do about it, squirt?' I was so mad, and the next day I caught Ricky in a quiet mood and decided to tell him about it. He was always running around, so communicating with him was not as easy as with Mom or Murray. But sure enough his thoughts came back to me and he said, 'those are fighting words. How big is he?' I described him with long legs, and almost twice my height.

Ricky didn't respond for a while and I wondered if he forgot about the topic. Then he opened his mouth and said out loud, "Ralph, how bad does it bother you? Maybe you should just move on to other things. You want to pick the battles you can win, and find work-arounds for the others. Let Branford have his silly marking."

Taking Ricky's advice, I ignore Branford. But come on, what kind of name is Branford? A mommas-boy from up north, or a couch-potato-lap-dog? Who names their dog Branford? I admit I don't know what 'up north' means but Mom says don't use that 'cause she's from St. Louis and some people around here have never left town and get confused about geography. So other than for Branford, I don't use that term. I do need to find out what 'geography' means, though.

~

I HEARD my name called out and as you might imagine it was the furry feline next door.

"Hey Ralph, I'm going to show you something that will make your day."

"Don't tell me. You knocked over Uncle Buck and he's now inhabiting the crevices and chinks on the hearth," I said.

"Very funny," he said. "Uncle Buck is still resting comfortably on the mantel. Come over closer and watch this."

He balanced himself on the top of the fence and began to shake all over. His head was zigging and his backend was zagging all at the same time like he was shaking a mouse off his back. Here we go, I thought, this is the end of Murray and a good friendship, nothing lasts forever... a seizure. I hope they give him a nice funeral.

Then he stopped and said, "Well, what do you think?"

"I think it's been nice knowing you and I'll look in on Uncle Buck when I can," I said.

"No, Ralph. I'm doing the Twist. It's a new dance and it's all the rage," he said.

"The rage?" I said.

"Everybody likes it. That's a rage," he said. "You twist yourself around to the music and the words and everybody has a ball. Ask Ricky to play the Chubby Checker song for you so you can hear the music. The words are cool, 'Daddy's sleeping and mamma's not around, we're going to twist all night till we tear the house down.'"

"You're going to do what?" I said.

"Not the house thing for real, just saying it for fun. 'You should see my little sis, she really knows how to rock, she knows how to twist,'" Murray continued.

I stood in awe and confusion. It's all come down to this. Murray has crossed over through the dark veil to the other side, I thought. Soon they'd be taking him away in a strait jacket...a small one, of course.

"Ralph, you have got to loosen up. You're stodgy, conservative life is boring. Open up, be real, get in the swing," Murray admonished. "Now stand evenly on all four legs and just move with the music."

"The music. What music?" I said.

"Just feel it in your soul. You don't have to actually hear it," he said. "Come on, Ralph, do me a favor; do yourself a favor; do the universe a favor; move baby, move."

I started swaying back and forth like Murray was doing.

"Okay, that's a good start," he said. "Feel the motion going to your back legs; round your bottom like you're drawing a circle on a page; let it flow."

The movement to my backend felt good, even fun. It was lifting my spirits; everything felt a little lighter. Things like the blue jay problem or Branford didn't seem as important.

"Look at that smile on your face," Murray gloated. "You're a twister, baby. You're in the groove. I get the feeling you're syncing with the thinking; you got the groove, on the move you're really turnin' on."

I figured Murray was hallucinating and I should exit the scene, but frankly I was having fun. Woody flew by, circled and on his second pass I shot him a message through the ether, 'it's the twist; get in the groove.'

On his third pass he said, "Anything I can do to help, I hope you make it back to normal sometime this summer."

I looked up to see Murray raise his bottom off the fence, move it back and forth, and then into a rounding motion, and then twist like crazy. The fence started to sway and believe me it was scary. I toned down my backend enough to make it to the patio, looked up to the fence and saw no cessation, just cat gone wild.

Okay then. What's for supper. I hope she puts the warm broth in the bowl over the dry food, I thought. A delicacy I call "chateau du chow."

~

ADMIT IT. If Murray said to you that your life was stodgy, it would hurt. Me too. I'm going to let it pass and move on to things I can control. Next a learning experience for the boys and a bit too much excitement for me. Buddy dropped by...you'll see. Read on.

CHAPTER 17

BEHIND THE COUCH

B uddy wheeled his bike into our driveway around ten that morning. It was summer and Tommy was away for two weeks at camp. Mom already left for a shopping trip, so it was just Ricky, Buddy, me, and Emma Dora. I'm not sure how the family would have gotten along without Emma. She came in three days a week, helped cleanup and do laundry, sometimes cooked meals, and best of all she made pies. The apple and cherry were highlights, but the tour d'force was the chess pie. I watched her make it one time. Crack some eggs, some butter, sugar and a touch of vanilla, and voila the food of the gods. At least that's what Dad called it.

Buddy walked in the house through the sliding door and back to Ricky's room. I slipped inside with him and quickly claimed my perch on Ricky's pillow, prepared for a morning of serious hanging-out. Ricky wore a tee shirt that said *Pope Taylor's BBQ* tucked into his camp shorts, and his most worn-out tennis shoes. Buddy never wore a tee shirt or worn-out anything. He donned a light-blue cotton shirt that buttoned up the front and at the collar, along with white club-shorts and leather shoes.

The talk was casual with a lot about Buddy's family of older sisters. The boys had been trying tennis and Ricky picked up his tennis racket and swung it around while they were talking, all the while Emma scurried back and forth in the hall.

The boys jumped up and headed to the living room. I knew where they were going...to the fort. The fort was a "secret place" behind the couch. The couch-back angled just enough against the wall that two small boys and a handsome puppy-dog could squeeze in. We had some crackers and two plastic six-shooter pistols stored there. But most of all, it was private and secret. The boys always whispered back there so nobody could find them. A sliver of light provided visibility for Buddy to reveal the small package that he scraped off the end-table as they entered the fort. Ricky knew what was in the package and when he saw it, he drug a small stick over the end of another box and the stick caught fire. Buddy sucked up the fire through his cigarette just the way Mom and Dad did, and the end lit up while smoke barreled out of his mouth. Ricky followed and within seconds the air was thick and hard to breath. I thought about crawling out, but didn't want to miss anything.

I didn't miss a thing because before the third puff Emma was screaming "fire, fire, everybody out of the house." The boys headed for open ground and I scooted out just ahead of them.

"Fire, fire, everybody out," Emma repeated.

By this time her voice was high pitched and hysterical. The boys brought their cigarettes out with them, but all Emma could see through the cloud by that time, was the fear in her own eyes.

The billows of smoke pouring from the couch started to dissipate when Mom burst through the back door to a screeching symphony of panic and apology. Emma's futile attempt to be heard over Ricky's apologetic screaming left the whole scene in chaos. The next thing I knew Buddy was on his bike rounding the curve of the driveway onto 4th Avenue.

If I were to mention Ricky was in the dog house for a couple of days it might sound quirky coming from me, but there's no better was to say it. He expected the worse and I could feel the angst and fear he was feeling around the time Dad was due home. Mom put Ricky in his room and said, "Don't you come out of here, MISTER. Your Dad will have a word with you when he gets home."

I snuggled in with him on his bed, and I think it made him feel better. When a quiet knock on the door happened, Ricky said. "Come in." We both looked up with no surprise to see Dad. I always knew that Dad was a gentle soul and I never heard him yell at another person. I felt a quiet resolve in him as I took a deep breath.

"Tell me about what was going on this afternoon," he asked.

Ricky rolled out the story and after he finished

his tale of the events Dad just said, "Do you feel it would be better to think through those things ahead of time? Be a little more responsible for what you do?"

Now that was a hard pill to swallow for me, because I can't remember ever thinking ahead about anything I do. I am only a dog, clever and witty, but still...a dog. I watched, though, as Ricky mulled over that advice and thought about it. He only replied to Dad, 'yes sir, I will next time.' It was a tepid response, but Dad seemed satisfied. He reached over and shook Ricky's hand, and said, 'we have a deal.'

Later after dinner around the kitchen table when it was just Mom and Dad, he told her that this was probably a good learning experience. Then he looked up and said, "Maybe we should quit smoking. It's probably not good for us and the kids learn to do what we do just by watching."

"Fine by me. I never liked the taste anyway," she replied.

FINE BY ME TOO. MY 'SNIFFER' is more sensitive than theirs, and that smoke was Yuki. Behind the couch was not my favorite fort anyway. Next, Elvis is singing my favorite song, and the Beach Boys are chiming in too. Sure, things got a little scary for a while, but when I settled down, I had time to reminisce about Buster and Woody. Jump into this one and you might agree that I saved the best chapter for last.

CHAPTER 18
THE CAR WASH

P ick up the dry cleaning, stop by the cobbler to drop off a pair of Dad's shoes, run by Miss Frankie's with a get-well card, grocery store; our last errand today was washing the car. Mom jumped out and last minute decided to leave me inside the car for the ride through.

The car door swung on its hinges cutting through the muggy, late-morning air and snapped into place with authority, closing me in with the grocery bags of flour, milk, peanut butter, sharp cheddar cheese, a couple of six-packs of Pepsi, and a pound of fresh Folgers coffee.

The clear water first hit the windshield rolling down in lines like little rivers flowing onto the dry, dusty hood. Then the soap started down in narrow streams that were quickly submersed in white suds flowing from above the car.

Elvis was delivering *Heart Break Hotel* through the speakers in a low drone, but the car wash

89

machines buzzed louder, so poor Elvis was losing his punch.

Inching over to the passenger side, I could see better without the steering wheel in the way, as the white suds turned to a mousy pink. Finally the clear water returned to cover the car and the suds rolled off of the light-brown metallic finish. The car slowly rolled onto the pavement and I saw Mom walk across the white concrete lot, reach out for the door handle and squeeze, but it didn't budge. Her elbow straightened and this time she yanked on the handle. Nothing. Her happy-go-lucky smile turned stern, and her eyes sunk a bit into their sockets.

I could see Mom's thoughts of frustration, and consternation. A man came over and she was talking at him fast, waving her right hand, then both arms expressing her urgency. The man threw up his hands in a "calm-down-lady" gesture. Then they both walked inside and were gone for a while. When Mom came back out, she walked up to the passenger door, bent her knees to be on my level and started talking to me. Her gaze was calmer and her thoughts were more resolved, but hearing any of her words was a challenge over the Beach Boys, *Help Me Rhonda*. After sitting on the curb next to me for a time, she walked over to the small building and went through the door.

I pawed a few times at the seat then scratched the surface—kind of like dogs do— before plopping down for the inevitable wait. That's when I saw them perched on the floorboard of the driver's side. Lying there innocent, benign and hiding, the keys.

Taking a deep breath, I started looking around. Did you know the radio has two knobs and one of them dials in stations? Of course you did, but I had never looked at it that closely. The dashboard and inside the doors are the same two-tone color as the outside paint—everything matching. I liked the driver's wheel, and of course, I already knew about the hand-crank for the widows, a little one for the "little window" and a bigger one for the main window, both silver with a black knob.

This time alone was hitting me between the eyes. The more I looked, the more I realized I never take the time to really see things. I'm always in a hurry to get in the car, go somewhere, get out of the car, make sure they don't forget me, bounce between Ricky and Tommy's lap. Am I taking the time to notice things around me? Am I caring enough about my friends and family?

Sometimes I am, like Dad with his stress, but do I show Mom how I feel about her, how much I notice that she makes everything run so smoothly? I wondered if I pay enough attention to the boy's feelings? Tommy is always concentrating on mechanical things and not so much on people. Should I be hanging with him more?

And what about Murray? He can be so frustrating and narrow and he never leaves his yard to see other things in the world, but it would be boring without him, and he taught me to twist. How good is that?

I looked up for Mom and a new set of keys, but she was nowhere in sight, as a gentle summer breeze rustled the leaves of the red oak tree next to the car. What about me and my dreams and aspirations? Am I striving to reach my full potential? Of all the friends I have in the yard and around town, how many can read? Woody is thoughtful and Buster, the little squirrel in the attic, is quite clever, but they can't read. I have special talents and what am I doing with it. Reading letters from Uncle Art? That's it. Is it enough to just exist on this planet, or is there a higher calling, one that elevates my peers and makes my yard and even the whole town better?

The radio was gurgling a bit and reception was on and off, but I could still make out Sam Cooke singing *Wonderful World*. What a special time to be alive, I thought! Resolving to re-think my life, starting today, I committed myself to being quiet and watchful and see everything around me every morning...before I start the day...take time to remember who my family is, who my friends are, and why I'm here now, in this town, with these friends and family. 'Mindful,' that's what I'll be.

I settled back in the driver's seat and took a deep breath. I hadn't felt that good in a long time, maybe ever. Yes my world was going to change and I was going to write my own story, starting today. Elvis singing *Hound Dog* rumbled through the speakers, while I nodded off to sleep.

"Ralph, hey Ralph," It was Mom knocking on the widow. "I'm back. We'll have you out of there in half a minute."

A man slid some sort of tool into the car at the top of the widow, snaked it down, yanked the little knob up, and the door flew open. Through the first crack of light I darted to the pavement and headed for the patch of grass under the big oak I'd been eyeing. I trotted back over to the car and Mom picked me up and held me tight, while I lavished her in dog kisses.

After dinner that night, I sat close to Mom watching *I Love Lucy*.

"Ralph won't let you out of his sight," Dad said.

"Well, we both had a big day," she said.

With the T.V. off, I made the rounds to make sure everybody was tucked into bed, then jumped up on the couch in the den and snuggled into the wool throw-blanket that always stayed there. I dug my nose into a fold of the blanket and thought about the events of the day. Then I said to myself, goodnight Dad, goodnight Mom, goodnight Tommy, goodnight Ricky, and finally goodnight Murray.

THE END

ABOUT THE AUTHOR

Rick Glaze published the kayaking adventure, *The Purple River* in 2021, *Spanish Pieces of Eight*, a sailing adventure/mystery, and *Jackass a Short Story Collection* in 2022. Rick was a financial columnist in Silicon Valley for San Francisco's *Nob Hill Gazette* and the *Los Altos Town Crier*. He attended the Stanford University Creative Writing Program, and is a graduate of Peabody College, Vanderbilt University, and MTSU. An award-winning songwriter, with a Pandora station and Spotify Playlist, credits on Country Music Television (CMT), and BBC Radio, Rick has rafted the Grand Canyon, the Salmon and Rogue Rivers as well as sailed throughout the Caribbean Sea. He hasn't sailed around Cape Horn, like the neighborhood character, Zeke, Ralph's friend down by the creek.

RICK'S PREMIUM READER CLUB

Join my Reader Club and be part of the excitement. I've enjoyed sailing and outdoor adventure for a long time and you can escape with me on these adventures by clicking below.

Get free books, free behind the scenes photos, original songs written for the books and more. Members are always first to hear about new offerings and publications. Click on *Rick's Guide to the Virgin Islands* at:

https://www.RickGlaze.com

Made in United States
North Haven, CT
03 May 2024

52058826R00065